Rascal

RUNNING FOR HiS LiFE

Collect all of Rascal's adventures:

Rascal

RUNNING FOR HIS LIFE

CHRIS COOPER

ILLUSTRATED BY JAMES DE LA RUE

EGMONT

EGMONT

We bring stories to life

First published in Great Britain in 2015
by Egmont UK Limited
The Yellow Building, 1 Nicholas Road, London W11 4AN

Text copyright © 2002 Chris Cooper
Illustration copyright © 2015 James de la Rue
The moral rights of the author and illustrator have been asserted

ISBN: 978 1 4052 7530 9

58626/1

www.egmont.co.uk

A CIP catalogue record for this title is available from the British Library

Typeset by Avon DataSet Ltd, Bidford on Avon, Warwickshire
Printed and bound in Great Britain by CPI Group

MIX
Paper
FSC FSC® C018306

For Judy and Art

CHAPTER 1

It wasn't the noise of passing traffic that woke Rascal. It wasn't the brightness of the morning sun either, as it peeked out from behind the clouds, or the breeze that rustled the leaves of the bushes around him.

No, it was better than that. It was
the smell of sausages. That and the
wonderful sizzle they made as they
cooked. To Rascal's ears it was one of
the best sounds in the world. It seemed
to whisper, 'Come and eat us, come and
eat us! What are you waiting for?'

When a dog is as hungry as Rascal
was, he doesn't need a second invitation.

The sun was already quite high.
Rascal had slept long after sunrise. He
had arrived in this town late the night
before. He was weak and exhausted
and there was a little blood between
the pads of one of his front paws. He

had just wanted to slump in the nearest doorway and sleep, but he knew that he couldn't do that. He'd tried that once before, a few towns back, and an angry shopkeeper had shooed him away first thing in the morning. It wasn't the greatest way to wake up. Rascal knew now that he had to find a better hiding place before he could allow the blackness of sleep to fold itself around him.

So, when all he'd wanted to do was curl up and close his eyes, the dog had forced himself to pad around this strange new town in search of a safe place. There was a small park near the square. Rascal had found a clump of bushes there and dug his way inside them. It wasn't very comfortable and it wasn't very warm, but that didn't stop Rascal from falling into a long dreamless sleep almost immediately.

The next thing he knew, it was morning and . . . that wonderful smell of sausages!

He wriggled forwards and peeked through the leafy branches. Like most dogs, Rascal's nose was a perfectly tuned food detector and it didn't take him long to spot where the smell was coming from – a hot dog stand just round the corner from the park.

Rascal was out of the bushes now. He gave his front paw a lick – it was still a little tender, but it wasn't hurting too badly this morning. Then he stretched his back legs out. He cocked his leg against a tree, and then turned his attention back to the hot dogs. His stomach was demanding immediate action!

The man at the stand was humming as he sliced bread rolls in half while a row of hot dog sausages cooked next to him.

Since he had been on his own, Rascal had learned that some people were happy to give a stray dog like him a bite to eat. For some reason, others got angry and started shouting at him. You could never know for sure which kind of person it would turn out to be.

Rascal approached the hot dog stand slowly and let out a hungry whimper. He didn't sit up and beg – his master, Joel, had no time for silly dog tricks like that – but the meaning was clear enough.

The man at the hot dog stand wasn't impressed. He flicked the dog nothing more than a bored glance.

'Scram,' he muttered.

So this man fell into the second group of people – the ones who *wouldn't* help Rascal on his long journey home.

Once, Rascal would have simply turned and left, but things were different now. He was starving and here was this glorious sizzle and smell!

Rascal began trotting casually along the pavement past the stand. He kept his eyes forwards and wagged his tail eagerly, as if he was concentrating on what lay directly ahead. He didn't even glance at the hot dog stand. The man didn't pay

much attention to the dog now, either.

Rascal had almost passed the stand when suddenly he whirled around and jumped up on to his hind legs. His front legs landed against the edge of the counter.

'Hey!' yelled the man angrily, but Rascal's head was already craning forwards. The sausages were hot, but it

was OK if he held them between his teeth and made sure that they didn't touch his tongue.

He managed to get two of them. He would have liked more, but there wasn't time. As soon as his front paws hit the ground again, he took off.

'You thieving dog!' shouted the man furiously.

Just the taste and smell of the food was enough to drive a hungry dog crazy. Rascal fought the temptation to wolf them down there and then. He raced into the park area. Now that he was running, his front paw had begun to

throb a little, but the thought of a hot
breakfast acted as powerful medicine.

A boy on a park bench laughed as the
dog streaked by him with two sausages
hanging out of its mouth. Normally
Rascal would have
stopped to say
hello to a friendly
face, but now
wasn't the time
for socialising.

Finally, Rascal slumped to the ground,
around the other side of a small building
in the park and out of sight of the hot
dog stand.

The first of the sausages was gone
in two snaps of his jaws. His tummy
gurgled gratefully. He took his time with
the second one. It was hard to say when
he would get the chance to eat again.
Better make sure he really enjoyed it.

The food was delicious, but there
was a part of the dog that wasn't happy
about getting breakfast this way. Back
when he was with his family, he had
always known that he wasn't allowed to
take food from the table. Oh sure, Joel
might take a bite or two of food from
his plate and feed it to Rascal under the
table. That was different. But Rascal had

learned as a puppy that, if he jumped up on to the table, someone – probably Joel's mum or dad – would frown and say, 'No! Get down!' The worst thing they would ever say – when the young Rascal had sampled the Christmas turkey the family was about to tuck into, for instance – was, 'Bad dog!'

Now there was no human around to say it to him, but the words still formed in the back of his mind: 'Bad dog!' Rascal put his head miserably on the grass.

Maybe he *was* a bad dog? It was a horrible thought, but why else would he be here, alone and so far from home? So far from Joel? A whimper escaped from the dog's throat as he thought once again about his master. What was Joel doing now? Was he thinking of Rascal?

Usually, Rascal was an observant dog, but all these thoughts of home stopped him noticing what was going on around him that morning. He didn't see the white van that pulled up alongside the park, or the man and woman that got out of it.

CHAPTER 2

What finally caught his attention was the piercing whistle. He looked up to see two people standing by the van. They wore identical green sweatshirts. The side door of the van was pulled open.

'Hey!' shouted the woman, looking right at Rascal. 'Want to go for a ride?'

She pointed to the inside of the van. Rascal could see an open cage with a blanket on the floor and a rubber chew-toy.

It looked nice and comfortable in there, but Rascal stayed put. His tail thumped with curiosity against the grass as the people began to walk towards him.

'It's OK, boy,' said the man in a voice that was trying hard not to sound threatening. He held out one hand. A doggy treat sat in his open palm – one of Rascal's favourites, too! A red lead dangled from the woman's hand.

'Here you are.' The man tossed the dog treat on to the grass between them.

'Breakfast time,' said the woman. Like the man, she spoke slowly and her voice was kind, but Rascal still held back.

Something wasn't quite right about this . . .

The man and woman had slowed down, but they were still walking, still getting closer and closer.

The wonderful smell of the treat filled Rascal's nostrils. His mouth began to water expectantly. More often than not, when there was one doggy treat, there were lots more where that came from!

He got to his feet and took a step forwards. But suddenly a gate in his mind opened and an old, old memory rushed through it. The hairs on the back of Rascal's neck rose.

Dog catchers! That's what these two were – dog catchers! If they caught him now, they would take him away in their white van.

Rascal only had a hazy memory of the place Joel and his family had taken him from when he was a puppy – more like a snippet of a dream than a real memory.

But one thing was certain: if these dog catchers took him back to a place like that, he would never see Joel again.

Once he understood this, the decision was made. He'd just have to live without the treat. Rascal swerved to the side and ran.

'Get him!' shouted the man, but his partner wasn't close enough.

'The collar-trap's in the van,' yelled the woman. The man nodded quickly and began to sprint back towards the parked vehicle. The woman ran after Rascal.

Usually the dog would have just run and kept on running. But the pads of his front left paw were hurting again. It was difficult to put much weight on the leg, and that meant it was difficult to run fast.

He turned on to a path that ran between a tennis court and a hedge. The woman followed, but she wasn't fast enough to catch him.

Rascal paused to give his bad paw a bit of a rest. He looked back at the woman, who was jogging towards him at a steady speed.

Suddenly, there was a noise up ahead of him. It was the man! He must have

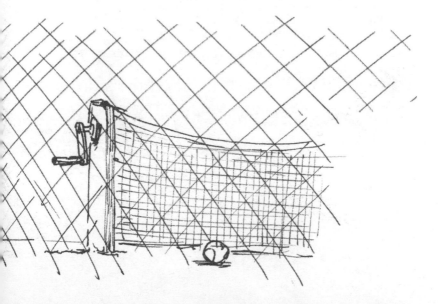

circled round the other way, and now he was on the path in front of Rascal. He held some sort of big loop in one hand.

The tennis court was surrounded by a mesh fence and the path was too narrow for Rascal to get past either of the dog catchers easily. There was nowhere to go – he was trapped.

But then he spotted a gap in the hedge. It was his only chance.

Rascal charged towards the man, who lunged forwards and flicked the loop in the dog's direction. It brushed the side of Rascal's neck, but it didn't go over his head. That was lucky because the man,

still holding the handle, released the thin end of the loop and it snapped down into a tight little circle.

If Rascal's head had been in there, he would be stuck now. Instead, the dog plunged through the gap in the shrubbery and into the dark tangle of roots that lay beyond it. Sharp branches scratched and clawed at him the whole way, but he barrelled his way through to the other side and crashed out on to another path.

What now? Up ahead was a children's playground. There was a row of swings to the side. The rest of the area was taken up by one big, multicoloured play structure. It didn't offer many hiding spots, but there was a slide that was completely covered. Rascal went to the bottom of it and jumped up. He tucked his back legs up so that he was hidden in the bottom section where the tube levelled off. No one would be able to see him unless they were directly in front of the hole at the bottom of the slide.

Rascal lay as still as he could. After a few moments, he heard the crunch of boots on gravel. The man and woman were in the playground.

'Where'd he go?' asked the woman.

'Beats me,' said the man. 'He can't have run so far. It looked as if his leg was hurting him.'

'Wait a minute,' said the woman. It sounded as if she was smiling.

Rascal held his breath in the silence that followed. Footsteps began to crunch on the gravel again. Were they going away? No, the footsteps were getting louder, closer!

'Have a look at this, Dan,' said the woman. Then she crouched down and said to the dog, 'You can't be comfortable in there.'

Rascal let himself be pulled out of the slide. The woman held one arm round his neck and shoulders. She was about to put the lead on him when a new voice shouted, 'There you are! Come here, boy!'

Rascal looked up. It was the boy from the park – the one who had been sitting on the bench. He was standing at the edge of the playground and holding out his arms as if he was waiting for Rascal to jump into them. As if he was Rascal's owner!

Confusion flashed through the dog's mind, but this had to be better than the

place the dog catchers would take him
to. Rascal bounded up to the stranger
and launched himself into the waiting
arms. The boy laughed as he staggered
under the impact of low-flying dog!

He was tousling Rascal's fur as if they were the best of friends. The two dog catchers joined them.

'Is this your dog?' asked the man.

'Yes, sir, he is,' answered the boy immediately.

CHAPTER 3

The two adults studied the boy suspiciously. The man jerked a thumb towards the dog.

'What's his name then?'

The boy hesitated only a fraction of a second: 'Flash.'

The dog catchers exchanged glances.

'Funny name for a dog,' said the woman.

The boy just shrugged.

'And you do know that your dog should be on a lead,' said the man sternly.

'With a collar and an ID tag,' added the woman.

The boy nodded in solemn apology. 'I know. He just got out of our house this morning – it was an accident. He didn't have his collar on 'cause we were going to give him a bath.'

'Looks like he needs a bath,' commented

the man, frowning at Rascal's matted
and dirty coat.

'And there's something wrong with his
front paw,' said the woman. 'You might
want to have a vet look at that.'

'We'll do that,' said the boy. 'And I'll take him home right now.'

The two adults thought it over. At last the woman said, 'OK, but I want you to write down your name and address for us.'

She held out a notepad and pencil. When the boy had finished writing, he clapped a hand against his leg.

'Heel, Flash,' he commanded, looking at Rascal. The words were strange, but Rascal knew what it meant when an owner patted his own thigh that way. He jumped up and stood at the boy's side.

'Thank you, and I won't let it happen

again,' said the boy, and then to Rascal, 'Come.' He walked briskly away and the dog trotted alongside. The two dog catchers didn't move. They stood and watched as boy and dog crossed the park.

When they were out of earshot, the boy smiled down at the dog and said in a friendly voice, 'You're doing brilliantly, pooch! But we need to get a bit further away before they realise I gave them the address of the pizza restaurant.'

The boy was a little older than Joel and he didn't really look much like him, and yet something about him reminded Rascal of his old master. It was something to do with the eyes, the way they seemed to smile and shine as if lit by the boy's kindness.

They turned a corner, then another. The boy looked back to see if the dog catchers were following. They weren't.

He knelt down to Rascal and rubbed the fur under his ears. 'OK, boy, you can go now!'

Rascal's brown eyes did not move from the boy's face. The rest of his body was just as still.

'Go on,' said the boy. 'Go home! I just don't like to see dogs caught and taken to the pound, that's all.'

Rascal didn't budge.

The boy rolled his eyes and began to walk away. The dog followed.

When he noticed his new shadow, the boy stopped and turned around.

'No!' he said firmly. 'You can't follow me home.' He made a shooing motion with one hand. 'Go on now. Go!'

Rascal sat patiently during this performance. Then, as soon as the boy turned and began to walk again, the dog resumed his trot, a few paces behind him.

The boy stopped once more.

'You don't get it, do you?' His voice
was getting high with frustration. 'You
can't follow me. Now go!'

Rascal just blinked and waited. The
boy opened his mouth to talk, but no
words came out. He just looked at
the dog. Finally, a smile replaced the
frustration in his eyes.

'I give in,' he groaned. Then he said

more quietly, 'You can come with
me, just for a little while. I'll give you
something to eat, OK? And I'll have a
look at that paw of yours. But you can't
stay.'

Sensing the boy's new tone of voice,
Rascal gave a little friendly bark.

'Yeah, right,' grinned the boy. 'You're
welcome.'

They walked on.

'What's your real name anyway? Is "Flash" OK?' asked the boy.

Rascal gave a couple of happy barks.

'Flash it is!' said the boy. 'It's from a TV programme I like! And my name's Lucas. I'd shake you by the paw –'

The laugh died in Lucas's throat. Rascal sensed the sudden shift in the boy's mood. For a moment it seemed as if he was about to turn and run away.

It was clear why. They were coming up to a line of shops set back from the road. In front of them was a square flowerbed nearly a metre off the ground.

Four or five teenagers were sitting on the low concrete wall around it.

The murmur of their conversation died when they spotted the boy and the dog. They all watched as Lucas walked closer. It was as if they were reeling him in with their unfriendly stares.

Rascal stuck close to his new friend. He didn't know what was going on, but something wasn't right here. He could sense it.

And it wasn't just the kids who were unfriendly. One of them held a brown dog on a short lead. This animal was powerfully built. Its shoulder and neck

muscles strained and bulged as it pulled
forward and a threatening growl gurgled
in its throat. It was the fiercest-looking
dog Rascal had ever seen.

One of the kids unfolded himself
from the wall and stood in Lucas's way.

This boy wasn't any taller than Lucas, but he was broader and seemed a year or two older.

'It's the new kid,' he said for the benefit of his mates. Then, with a sneer to Lucas, 'Hello, new kid.'

'My name is Lucas,' said Rascal's friend. The boy's voice was quiet, but Rascal could hear the anxious thudding of his heart.

The older boy smiled but it was a forced, deliberate smile without any warmth of friendship. It didn't reach his eyes, which remained a cold slate-grey.

'And what are you doing here, *Lucas*?'

It wasn't a friendly enquiry.

'I'm staying with my dad,' he said softly.

'I've seen him around before, Jed,' called one of the seated kids. 'His dad's a couple of blocks away from our house. The kid was here last summer too.'

'Yeah,' said another, 'he does odd jobs, gardening and that. I saw him working over on the posh side of town.'

The boy called Jed nodded approvingly.

'Is that right?' he said. He leaned in closer. 'That's great, Lucas! In fact, I could probably help you out. Help you

to find some
new clients
or something.
All it would
cost you is
. . . oh, about
twenty-five
dollars.'

'I don't need your help, thank you,'
said Lucas.

Jed's smile stretched thin. 'I don't think
you're following me here,' he snarled.
The false smile was still on his face, but
his voice was hard and cold. 'See, I'm
not asking you. I'm *telling* you.'

He glanced around at his cronies, who were all grinning. 'Get that money to me, or your summer visit here is going to be a nightmare. *Now* do you get it?'

Rascal didn't pay much attention to this exchange. He had worries of his own. The brown dog's iron gaze hadn't budged from him for an instant. Rascal was generally a friendly dog – he hardly ever got into fights with other dogs and he had *never* been the one to start a fight – but this dog was like no other he had ever encountered. It acted as if its whole purpose in life was to rip Rascal to pieces.

The brown dog let out a sudden vicious bark. Something chilling and savage echoed in that deep bark, but Rascal refused to back down. Instead he gave a bark in return.

The boy holding the other dog's lead laughed. 'You'd better watch out, Lucas,' he smirked. 'Looks like that dog of yours fancies its chances, but no dog alive can go up against a dog like Slammer. Especially not a mutt.'

'Yeah,' agreed one of the other kids.

'Slammer would make mincemeat out of it.'

'Slammer would make *dog* food out of it, you mean,' said the boy called Jed. The harsh chorus of laughs got louder.

Lucas and Rascal began to walk away.

'You'd better not forget what I said,' came a voice behind them.

Neither boy nor dog looked back. They walked the rest of the way to Lucas's house in silence.

CHAPTER 4

Lucas led Rascal up the driveway of a small, single-storey house. The patch of grass in front of the house wasn't big, but it was trim and tidy.

A door was open on the side of the house. Before he reached it, Lucas turned to the dog.

'Wait here, boy,' he said. 'And no barking, please.'

Rascal wasn't sure what the boy wanted, but then he said, 'Sit!'

That was more like it. It was good to have a clear-cut instruction again. Rascal immediately sat, and the boy disappeared through the side door.

Rascal heard the sound of voices through the window.

'It's just me,' called Lucas.

'Hi, Lucas,' said a man's voice. He sounded distracted, as if he wanted to be concentrating on something else.

Rascal's ears caught the rustle of newspaper.

'What's going on, Dad?' Lucas asked.

'Same as usual. I'm just seeing what jobs there are in the newspaper,' came the answer.

'And? Is there anything?'

'Not yet, son. Not yet.' The voice was friendly, but Rascal detected a note of tiredness and worry in it.

Outside, Rascal was still sitting but he had inched forward to peep through the screen door into the house. Lucas was kneeling at the fridge, but he wasn't really paying much attention to its contents. Instead he was looking at the man who sat at the kitchen table.

Lucas's father was staring intently at the newspaper spread wide before him. He held a pen in one hand. Every so

often he drew a ring round something on the page.

Lucas cleared his throat. 'Dad, I know you've got a lot on your mind, but there's something I want to talk to you about . . .'

Rascal could hear the anxiety in Lucas's voice, but the boy's father could not. He took out his phone. 'That's great, buddy,' he said. 'But can we talk about it this evening? I've really got to make a few phone calls about these jobs. The early bird gets the worm and all that.'

He began dialling, reading the number

from the folded newspaper in his hand.

Lucas sighed to himself and turned back to the fridge.

'Hello?' his dad was saying into the phone. 'Yes, I'm calling about the job that is in today's paper.'

As he spoke, he turned towards the screen door. Rascal pulled his head back out of sight quickly. He listened to the man's voice for the next couple of minutes. But another noise from the house was more interesting to him. It was the clatter of crockery. That meant one thing – food!

The side door opened again. Lucas

appeared with two bowls in his hands. He was also carrying a small bottle and a cloth.

He sat down with his back against the wall and put the bowls down.

'First things first,' said Lucas. 'Let's have a look at that paw. Then we can eat lunch.'

It was good for the boy to pay attention to something other than his own worries. He gently took Rascal's paw in his hand and began to look between the pads. It was painful

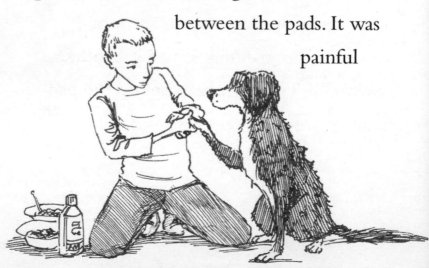

and at one point the dog couldn't stop himself from yanking his leg back.

'Sorry,' said Lucas. Slowly Rascal put his paw out again.

'Here's the problem,' said Lucas after another minute. 'There's something stuck in here. A thorn maybe.'

He tried to get the object out with his finger and thumb. For an instant pain stabbed up Rascal's leg, but then Lucas was holding a tiny object triumphantly in front of him.

'Got it,' he grinned. 'It's a bit of glass. Now all I have to do is clean up the pad a bit.'

He poured a little liquid from the bottle on to the cloth. 'This might sting a little,' he said. 'That's what my mum always says when something is going to sting a *lot*!' He gently dabbed the cloth on to Rascal's paw. It *did* sting a lot, but Rascal didn't bark or whimper.

'Well done,' said Lucas, reaching for the two bowls. 'Now we can eat lunch.'

The dog noticed that the boy had the same food in his own bowl. Lucas began shovelling it into his mouth with a fork.

'Don't ask what it is,' said the boy. 'Leftovers.'

Rascal began to chomp on the meat.

He could have done without the bits of tomato in it and there was something hot in the food that left an odd burning sensation in his throat. Then again, he wasn't really in a position to be a picky eater. He wolfed the lot down and licked the bowl.

'Wow!' smiled Lucas. 'I guess that hit the spot, huh?'

The boy was just finishing his lunch – with Rascal eyeing every single mouthful – when a woman appeared at the top of the drive. Lucas jumped up and stopped her before she reached the front door.

'Can I help?' he asked.

The woman was carrying a clipboard and a plastic collection box. 'Yes,' she said. 'Is your mother or father around?'

Lucas shook his head. 'My dad's here, but he's busy,' he answered.

'Is your mother in?'

Lucas held up one arm to shield his eyes from the sun. 'My mother doesn't live here,' he said. 'My mum and dad split up years ago. I live with my mum most of the time but I come here in the summer.' He stopped, as if he was suddenly aware that he was talking too much about this.

'So . . . can I help you?' he asked.

The woman indicated her collection box. 'I'm collecting for the community centre on Monroe Street. We need a new roof, among other things.'

Lucas pulled a handful of change from his pocket and put it in the slot.

'It's all I've got on me,' he said apologetically.

The woman smiled. 'That's very kind. Every little helps,' she said. 'Thank you.'

She began to leave, but turned back. There was a look of concern in her eyes.

'When will your father be free?'

'Don't know. He lost his job a couple

of months ago. He's looking for a new one.'

The woman's face was sympathetic. 'What does he do?' she asked.

'He can do pretty much anything,' said the boy with an edge of pride in his voice. 'He built this house himself, before I was born.' He glanced back towards it. 'I was only here until I was four. I don't remember it very well from then.'

The woman smiled. 'Well, I wish him the very best of luck.' She shook the collection box. 'And thank you!'

She headed off for the next house.

Lucas picked up the two empty bowls. Then he glanced at his watch and his eyes bulged with surprise.

'I'm going to be late,' he gasped and charged back inside. He quickly set the two bowls in the sink and shouted to his dad, 'I'm going.'

His dad had just finished one phone call, but the telephone was still in his hand for the next. 'OK . . . er, where to?'

'Mrs Walker's. I do her garden today.'

His dad nodded, but it was clear that he wasn't really listening to what his son had to say. Then he spoke into the phone: 'Hello. Is there someone I can talk to about the job in the paper?'

Back outside, Lucas grabbed his bicycle from the back of the house. He rode to the top of the drive, then stopped and looked around at Rascal. The dog was eyeing him expectantly.

'Well? Are you coming or what?' asked the boy.

Rascal scrambled happily to his feet.

CHAPTER 5

Lucas stayed on the pavement and rode
slowly so that the dog could keep up
with him.

For Rascal, this was wonderful. Even
though his legs ached – they always
ached these days – there was something

different about trotting along behind this boy who reminded him so much of Joel. His paw felt different now – it was still sore, but it no longer seemed as if it was only going to get worse. Now he just needed to take it easy and the paw would be fine again.

After they had turned a few corners, the neighbourhood started to look different. It was a gradual change, but it seemed as if everything was getting bigger – the houses, the gardens, the expanses of lawn in front, the cars. The trees that arched over the street here were old and leafy.

Lucas stopped at a big wooden house.

It was set back from the pavement by a large front garden with a lawn and pretty flowerbeds.

Lucas leaned his bike against the fence.

'You'd better stay here,' he said to Rascal. 'There's some shade under the tree.'

Rascal picked out the key word from the boy's comments: 'stay'. He flopped to the ground obediently, then watched as Lucas went up to the front door.

For a while it seemed as if no one was in, but Lucas waited patiently on the doorstep. At last, an elderly woman appeared. She had a pair of glasses halfway down her nose and a battered paperback book in her hand.

She smiled when she saw the boy. 'Lucas! Is it Saturday again?'

'Yes, Mrs Walker.'

'I suppose it must be. Well, the garage is open. And you know where everything is, don't you?'

Lucas nodded.

'Good, good. Well then, I'll leave you to your work.'

Rascal watched as Lucas went to the garage at the side of the house. He reappeared with a lawnmower. He pulled the cord on it and the splutter of its engine drowned out the sound of birds and bugs.

From the pavement, Rascal could see only part of the back garden. Lucas walked in and out of view as he mowed the lawn. After that, he started to trim the borders of the lawn. The sun was

hot and soon Lucas's shirt was wet with perspiration. Beads of sweat glistened on his forehead.

After he'd put the lawnmower back into the garage, he began to weed the garden. Lucas had the unusual knack of becoming completely absorbed in what he was doing. He was totally focused on the job. What's more, he really seemed to enjoy it. He didn't just attack the garden as if it were his enemy. He made sure he did a thorough job.

At one point he stopped and lifted his arm up for a closer look at something that was on his wrist. He put his lips together and blew gently. The ladybird on his arm took to the air and wobbled away to another part of the garden.

Lucas had been working for about an hour when Mrs Walker came out of the side door. She was holding a tray with a tall glass of lemonade. Its sides were lined with drops of condensation and the ice in the glass made a wonderful clinking sound.

'Thought you might need a glass of lemonade,' she said.

'Yes, please,' said Lucas enthusiastically. He set his hoe to one side and took the glass. One gulp later, half the drink was gone.

'I notice you didn't come alone today,' said Mrs Walker. She gestured towards the front of the house.

'I take it that's your dog?'

'Sort of,' Lucas answered carefully. 'I mean, he's with me but he isn't exactly my dog. It's just —'

'I understand,' said Mrs Walker. 'But I'm not sure that's the best place for him.

Besides, I think he might need a drink in this hot sun, don't you?'

'I guess so. I . . . thought you might not like it if there was a strange dog in your back garden.'

'Not at all! I think you'd better call him over and I'll go and find a bowl,' said Mrs Walker.

A minute later Rascal was at the back of the house slurping up water from a bowl on the grass. It felt fantastic. He couldn't drink the icy liquid quickly enough. The tips of his ears dipped into it, but he didn't care.

Mrs Walker laughed as she watched him.

'That's just how my dog used to drink,'
she said.

'I didn't know you had a dog,' said
Lucas, setting his glass back on the tray.

'Oh, a good few years ago,' said Mrs
Walker. 'Her name was Lucy. She was an
Afghan hound.'

'One of those dogs with all the long hair?' asked Lucas.

'Those are the ones,' said Mrs Walker. 'Don't get one unless you want to spend half of your day brushing and grooming.' She smiled fondly at the memory.

'You know,' she said at last, 'I think I might still have one of Lucy's old collars in the basement. Your dog really ought to have a collar on. Would you like me to try and find it?'

'Er . . . OK,' answered Lucas.

A few minutes later Mrs Walker was putting the collar round Rascal's neck. It was a fancy leather one. Even on the last hole it was still a bit big for him, but it felt good to have a collar on again . . . as if he were more than just a stray, even if the name on the tag wasn't his own.

Mrs Walker stood back to admire the collar. 'Very handsome,' she said. 'Well, at least it'll do for the time being, won't it?'

Rascal gave a proud bark.

Mrs Walker grinned and then said to Lucas, 'But I mustn't keep you from your work.'

She disappeared inside the house. Rascal settled into a patch of sunlight on the grass and half-closed his eyes, as Lucas returned to work. The dog was comfortable here, with the warmth of the sun on his back and the lazy chirp of crickets in the distance. Finally, his eyes closed to slits and Rascal was content to let sleep just carry him off on its gentle currents.

He woke with a start as the screen door at the side of the house slammed shut. It was Mrs Walker again. She opened the door of the car in the driveway.

'I tell you, I would forget my head if it weren't screwed on,' she said to Lucas, who was tugging at the roots of a particularly stubborn weed. 'I clean forgot that I have an appointment this afternoon. How much longer do you have to go, Lucas?'

'I've just got to tidy up and take the weeds round the back of the garage,' said the boy. 'About fifteen minutes.'

Mrs Walker did a quick calculation in her head and unsnapped her purse.

'Here you are,' she said, holding out some money. Lucas wiped the soil from his hands on to his jeans to take it.

'And I'll see you next week!' she added, with a brisk wave.

Then she jumped into her car and backed out of the driveway. She beeped the horn once in farewell, and then she was gone. It was only then that Rascal noticed something lying on the drive. He gave it a sniff, but it was nothing edible and so not very interesting, as far as he was concerned.

'Whatcha got there, Flash?' asked the boy. He bent down to pick the object up.

Suddenly
his eyes
opened
wide in
surprise. It
was a roll of
banknotes.

'They . . . they must have fallen from
Mrs Walker's purse,' Lucas said. He
seemed to be holding his breath and, in
a way, the world around him seemed to
be doing the same. Lucas ran his finger
across the edge of the notes so that they
flicked back with a satisfying snapping
sound.

The boy looked as if a terrible weight had landed on him. Rascal couldn't know it, but one had. Of course Lucas knew what was the right thing to do. This had to be Mrs Walker's money, hadn't it? So, there was a letterbox set into the front door – it would be easy enough just to pop the money through there. He didn't have any pen or paper to write a note of explanation, but she'd be able to figure out what had happened. But . . .

'Just look at this house,' the boy said aloud to Rascal. 'I mean, she doesn't *need* the money. She won't even *miss* it, not really . . .' His hand closed around the money. 'And what if she'd dropped it in town instead of here? Someone would just pocket it, wouldn't they? They wouldn't even know it was hers . . . Bet they wouldn't hand it in at the police station or anything like that.'

Lucas sounded as if he was trying to persuade someone – himself. He bit his lower lip nervously. 'I . . . I could just *borrow* it. By the end of the summer I'd pay it all back. That'd be OK, wouldn't it?'

Of course, Rascal gave no answer.

Finally, Lucas turned away from the

dog's steady gaze and thrust the money into his pocket.

'OK,' he said, still not looking into the dog's eyes. 'I've got to finish up here.' He turned and began to push the wheelbarrow towards the end of the garden.

CHAPTER 6

The ways of humans were often a
mystery to Rascal, as they are to all dogs
at one time or other. But dogs are highly
aware of the moods and emotions of
their masters. It was clear to Rascal that
Lucas was troubled.

As the boy rode back to his own house, he was silent. He didn't look back once to check if Rascal was keeping up with him. A worried look remained in his eyes the whole way home.

Back at the small house, there was no sound from indoors. The back door was shut now – no one was at home. Lucas leaned his bike against the wall and led Rascal round the back.

'Sit,' he whispered, pushing down the dog's hindquarters, then, 'Stay.'

Lucas was in the garage for a minute or two. He reappeared carrying a length of thin rope.

He tied one end on to the new collar round Rascal's neck. He tied the other end round a drainpipe at the back of the house.

'You . . . you can't come with me this time,' said Lucas. His eyes still avoided Rascal's. 'I . . . I don't want you anywhere near that horrible attack dog again.' The guilty look in his eyes suggested another reason: Lucas didn't want anyone to see what he was about to do.

Rascal tried to lick the boy's face, but Lucas reared back.

'No,' he hissed. Then, more gently, 'You've got to be quiet back here, do you understand?'

Lucas got on to his bike.

'I'll be back soon,' he said. 'OK?' And

then he was gone.

But it wasn't OK. Of course, Rascal didn't understand the boy's words, but he knew that something was very wrong. Why else would the boy seem so nervous? Why else would he have been blinking back tears as he rode away?

Something was not right.

Rascal scratched at the collar with a front paw, trying to slip it over his head. That didn't work. Nor did backing up and trying to tug his head out of it.

He tried gnawing on the rope. It gave a little, but it was too strong. It would take him ages to chew through it. That wasn't going to work either.

What could he do? The answer came in the sound of a car door slamming from round the front of the house. There was nothing else for Rascal to do. The dog threw back his head and let out a howl, then another louder one. He just had to hope that the person from the car would hear and come to check out the din.

It took quite a few howls before someone appeared at the corner of the house. It was Lucas's father.

He was wearing smarter clothes than the
T-shirt and jeans he had been wearing
in the kitchen earlier.

A puzzled look came over the man's
face when he saw Rascal.

'Lucas!' he shouted into the house
through a partially opened window.
'What's this dog doing here?' There was
no answer from inside. 'Lucas, are you in
there?'

When he was sure that his son wasn't
around, Lucas's dad approached Rascal.

The dog let out another sound – half-
howl, half-yelp. He shook his head from
side to side as if in pain.

'Is that rope hurting?' said Lucas's dad with a frown. When he was closer, Rascal could see that this man had the same look of kindness in his eyes that his son had. He let Rascal sniff his hand to get used to him, then he bent down and started to untie the knot in the rope. He kept one arm round the dog, but his grip loosened a little when he came to retie the rope to the collar.

It was the only chance he would get, and Rascal took it. He yanked his shoulders back out of the man's grip.

'Hey!' exclaimed Lucas's dad in surprise.

But there was nothing the man could do.
He stood with the end of the rope in
one hand and just watched as the dog
zipped up the driveway and

out on to the pavement.

Rascal ran in the direction Lucas had taken, but the boy wasn't in sight. He had been gone a few minutes. How could Rascal find him?

At first, it wasn't so hard because there was only one direction he could go in. But then the road ended in a T-junction. Lucas could have gone either way.

Rascal stopped at the corner and looked both ways. There was no sign of the boy at all. How was he going to find him now? Panic began to tug at Rascal's heart.

CHAPTER 7

Should he just leave now, keep on moving west? No, whatever was going on, this boy who had befriended him was in trouble. He couldn't leave – not yet.

Rascal stood and closed his eyes. He

lifted his nose and sniffed deeply. A dog's sense of smell is many, many times more sensitive than a person's. As usual, the world was a jumble of smells to Rascal – the scent of a cat that had passed this way in the last twenty minutes, the bitter smell of car fumes, the smell of cooking from a nearby kitchen, the sickly-sweet fragrance of flowers in the garden near him.

And in the middle of it all, there was Lucas's scent, very faint but nonetheless there. As with every human, it was as unique and unmistakable as a set of fingerprints.

Now Rascal forced himself to ignore all the other smells bombarding his nose. He concentrated only on that one scent. It was like focusing attention on a single blade of grass in the middle of an entire lawn.

He trotted to the right, slowly at first but then gaining speed.

Every so often he would hit a patch where he couldn't detect the scent at all. He nearly gave up a few times. But he stayed calm, and eventually his nose caught the scent again.

The trick was to think with your nose.

Every time he came to a corner, he stopped and took his time, almost tasting the air with his snout.

Finally he came to a part of the town he knew – the park, the one he had spent the previous night in. And there was Lucas!

The boy was on the far side of the park. He was getting off his bike and

leaning it against the fence. He looked at his watch nervously. Rascal realised that Lucas was waiting to meet someone here.

Rascal tried to speed up, but his paw was beginning to hurt him again. All he needed to do was rest it for a while, but that wasn't going to be possible. Instead he leaned to one side to compensate for the ache. That was probably the only reason why he saw the dog hurtling across the grass towards him. It was the one he had seen this morning, Slammer, the vicious-looking dog that had seemed so eager to fight.

Now it had its chance. Far behind it, the dog's owner, the same boy Rascal had seen that morning, was running as fast as he could. The vicious dog was dragging its lead through the grass behind it. Had it pulled itself free of its owner's grasp? The alternative was even worse. Had the boy simply let go of the lead?

It didn't make much difference now. The stocky dog hurtled towards him like a rocket . . . a rocket with teeth.

Rascal got ready to defend himself, but a sudden dread gripped him as he looked at his attacker. Most dog fights

were a matter of establishing who was the boss, of putting another animal in its place. There was usually plenty of barking and snarling and there were sometimes bites but, more often than not, no dog was badly injured. Once it became clear who was going to win, both sides stopped.

But just one look at this dog made something very clear – it would never stop. This muscular dog lived for fighting and nothing else; its owner had made that much clear. It didn't even bark or growl as it raced forwards. Somehow that grim-faced silence was scarier than the fiercest of barks.

In an instant it was clear to Rascal what he had to do – the only thing he could. He turned and ran. There was nothing else for it. He ran for his life.

Usually he would have been confident that he could outdistance the dog chasing him – Rascal's legs were longer and he was younger. But everything was different today. The ache in his front paw slowed him down. The tiredness in his bones, after days on the road, slowed him down still further.

But he forced himself to go faster, dashing across the road and round the corner. He glanced back. Perhaps the dog hadn't followed him across the road, perhaps . . .

No, the telltale scrape of paws on the pavement was followed by the sight of the brown dog charging round the corner.

Rascal gulped more air and ran on, forcing himself to ignore the throbbing pain in his paw.

Perhaps there was a fence that he could jump over – one that was too tall for the other dog? That might allow him to make his escape . . . but there was nothing he could see. The panting of the dog's breath behind him was growing louder.

Rascal was getting exhausted now. He reached a metal bike rack outside a large building. There was space for five bikes to be locked up, but only one was there at the moment.

Rascal knew that he had to stop, but at least this bike rack would serve as a good barrier. If he could just keep it between himself and his pursuer . . . he only needed a minute or two to catch his breath.

The other dog raced up to the bike rack. Instead of choosing to go round

it one way or another, it simply leapt at the rack, aiming to jump through a gap between the bars in the middle of the metal structure. The gap was just about wide enough for the attacker's head to fit through.

All Rascal saw was a fearsome pair of jaws coming his way. They closed with a SNAP on ... nothing at all! The dog jerked backwards and landed on its side with a thud. It was back on its feet in a flash, but it wasn't able to reach its prey.

The end of its lead had become hooked over a metal bar that jutted out at the bottom of the bike rack!

A terrible rage gripped the
dog. It kept
on leaping
forwards,
but each
time the
lead snapped
taut and then jerked the dog back.

Rascal padded just a little way away
from the dog. He should have just kept
on, but he couldn't help himself. He
looked back and stared straight into the
brown dog's eyes. He didn't bother to
bark loud or long. Just one unhurried
yip was enough.

The dog went crazy at this gesture, but Rascal just carried on padding away, taking care not to put too much weight on his bad paw. He ignored the enraged snarls and barks behind him.

But then Rascal heard a different noise – a ripping sound, as the stitching in the handle of the lead came loose and the vicious dog tumbled on to the ground.

It was free again!

CHAPTER 8

Exhaustion and terror battled inside Rascal. The terror won out, but only just. He ran again. His tongue was hanging out of his mouth now as he sucked in air. How much longer could he keep this up? The dog didn't show any signs of tiring. How much longer before it caught up with him? And then what?

The whole world became a blur. It moved with the slowness of a frightening nightmare. Everything carried on as usual around him, apparently unaware of the terrible struggle that was going on right here.

But then something seemed to stand out of the blur he was running through. It took Rascal a moment to place the memory, but then he had it. It was the white van, the one driven by the dog catchers who had almost caught him in the park.

The van was parked now outside a shop. The woman sat in the driver's seat, while the man was inside the shop buying something.

The woman hadn't spotted Rascal, but that wasn't hard to change. He didn't stop running, but Rascal lifted his head and barked as loudly as he could. It was a ragged, frantic sound.

He didn't even have time to notice whether the dog catcher had noticed him. He was nearing the end now . . . He limped across the street and into a narrow alleyway.

Rascal was several steps inside it before he realised that the alley was a dead end, leading to a mesh fence that was far too high to jump over. It was too late to turn back to the entrance now. The only thing he could do was run on. As he did, he checked to see if any of the doors that led from the back of the buildings on to the alley were open. None were.

He reached the fence at the far
end. Perhaps he could dig a hole,
squeeze himself under? He tried,
but it was no good. His claws
scrabbled against solid concrete.

Rascal turned and looked back down
the alley. The dog was halfway. It was
taking its time now, striding
powerfully towards Rascal.
This was it. Rascal
took a deep
breath.
At least he
would do
his best.

He would put up a good fight.

Suddenly he noticed movement at the far end of the alley – the dog catchers! A tiny seed of hope sprouted in his heart.

The dog catchers were moving quickly, half-crouching and half-running and doing their best not to make too much noise. The man was holding the long stick-thing with a loop on the end.

He brushed against a rubbish bin. To Rascal the clatter it made was deafening, but the dog still didn't look around. Its whole attention was focused on Rascal. Meanwhile, the dog catchers continued to sneak up behind it.

By the time the dog did notice them, it was too late. The man in the green sweatshirt slid the end of the snare-trap round the dog's neck. He pulled the wire at the other end of the stick and the loop closed tight.

Immediately, the dog began to shake and jerk its head furiously. From the way the man had to hold on, it was clear that

the animal was incredibly strong. The
stick was almost wrenched free from his
grasp, but he just about managed to hold
on to it.

The struggle went on for a long time,
but at last even the dog realised that its
efforts were futile. It stopped fighting
and settled for glaring at its human

captor and letting out an occasional snarl.

'I can't believe someone would let a dog like this out on its own,' said the woman.

'Neither can I,' agreed the man, catching his breath. 'Dangerous dogs like this ought to be kept under control at all times. It's not the dogs that I blame – it's the *owners*.'

'Well, someone's going to have a hefty fine to pay,' said the woman with a fierce, tight-lipped smile.

The two adults turned their attention to Rascal.

'We'd better get this one, too,' said the

man. 'It probably doesn't even know what a close shave it just had.'

'I'm not so sure,' said the woman. She stepped closer to the trembling dog.

'Wait a minute,' she said. 'We saw this one before, didn't we? In the park, this morning.'

The man nodded. 'At least it has a collar on now. But where's the owner?'

The woman's hand was close to Rascal now.

'It's OK, boy,' she said reassuringly. But Rascal edged backwards, pressing himself against the fence. He knew that these people didn't mean him any harm, but he knew too where they would take him if they did catch him. It all added up to one thing – however tired he might be, he wasn't done running yet.

Digging up a last burst of energy, Rascal rushed forward, dodging left to avoid the woman.

'Get him!' yelled the man.

The funny thing was, the woman *could* have got him. Her hand was close enough to just reach out and grab Rascal by the collar. But for some reason she hesitated. When he remembered this moment afterwards, Rascal wasn't sure why – could she have felt sorry for him?

Whatever the woman's reasons, the second's delay was all Rascal needed. He zigzagged past the second dog catcher, keeping well away from the trapped dog, and hurtled back out of the alley.

He ran past the dog's owner, who was running down the street.

'Hey, where's Slammer?' the boy asked as Rascal rushed by him. He wasn't

aware yet of the trouble he would soon be in. Hah!

Rascal ran on, forcing himself to ignore the throb of pain in his paw. He could see the park now. Lucas and the older boy called Jed were there, facing each other. Lucas reached into his pocket and pulled out a couple of banknotes. A grin spread across Jed's face as he held his hand out.

It hurt, but Rascal picked up speed. He let out an urgent bark and ran out into the road.

There was a squeal of car brakes and the angry beep of a horn. A car had almost hit him!

'What are you
doing, you stupid dog?'
yelled a voice from the wound-
down front window.

The car drove off, but now the two
boys were both looking at Rascal
running towards them. Lucas opened his

eyes in alarm at how the dog looked.

'Flash!' he cried. 'What's wrong?'

He knelt down and hugged the dog tight, squeezing him to his neck.

When he stood again there were hot tears of anger in Lucas's eyes. He thrust the money back into his pocket. Seeing the dog's bravery, he had remembered his own.

'This isn't yours,' he said defiantly.

Jed's grin didn't fade. 'I don't know what you think you're doing, but you're making a big mistake,' he said, his voice heavy with threat. He clenched his fists.

Before Lucas could respond, Rascal

did. He bared his teeth and let out a low growl. It was full of anger, not just at this boy, but anger at being tired and alone and far from home.

Jed took a step back.

'No, YOU'RE making a big mistake if you think you can bully money out of me,' said Lucas.

'That's OK *now*, when you've got your dog with you,' sneered the older boy. 'But it won't always be with you, will it?'

Lucas didn't flinch. 'I don't need a dog to help me. I'm not afraid of you any more, Jed. You can just leave me alone.' What's more, Jed could see that these were not empty words. There was a new strength in Lucas's voice.

Lucas looked down at Rascal. 'Come on, Flash,' he said. 'Let's get this money back where it belongs.'

CHAPTER 9

When they got back to Lucas's house, his dad was standing anxiously at the front window.

He spotted his son wheeling his bike down the street and ran out to meet him.

Lucas's eyes were still red. His voice
almost choked in his throat as he looked
at his father.

'Dad,' he said. 'There's something I
have to tell you.'

Lucas's father smiled. 'That's good, son,' he said. 'Because I really want to talk to you, too.'

He swept his son up in a big hug.

'For one thing,' laughed Lucas's dad, 'there's the small matter of who exactly this dog is and what it was doing in our back garden!'

★　★　★

The sun was sliding down again, but Rascal felt much more comfortable now than he had the previous night. He was lying in Lucas's back garden listening to the boy and his father talk and laugh as they threw a baseball back and forth. The dog's belly was full and he could hear sleep begin to call to him from deep down somewhere.

The rest of the day played back in his mind.

Lucas and his father had sat down at the kitchen table, and this time his dad had really listened while Lucas told him everything about Jed and Mrs Walker's money. The boy had looked shame-faced. His gaze didn't move from the tabletop the whole time. When he was done, his dad put a hand on his shoulder.

'I'm the one who should apologise, Lucas. I'm sorry I didn't let you tell me earlier and I'm sorry for the way I've been,' he said. 'It's just . . . it's been hard. Trying to find work has been such a worry, and . . . when I lost my job, your mother thought maybe you shouldn't come out here this summer, you know, until I found something else. But I told her it would be fine . . .' His voice trailed off. 'I'm glad you've been here with me. I'm always glad of that.'

'So did you go to a job interview this afternoon?' asked Lucas.

'Yeah, but no luck.' Despite this, a little

smile was playing on his dad's face.

'What is it?'

'Ah well, there was some news waiting for me when I got home,' said Lucas's dad. 'Seems they need a handyman at the community centre on Monroe Street. They heard about me and someone telephoned to talk about the job. You wouldn't know anything about that, would you, son? Hmm?' He ruffled Lucas's hair. 'It's only for a few weeks, but that'll be enough for me to find a full-time job. I think we're going to be OK.' He looked at Rascal, who was sitting in the corner. 'Right, boy?'

Rascal wasn't sure of all that had been said, but he replied with an enthusiastic bark.

Before dinner, Lucas called Mrs Walker. He made his way through the same explanation, stammering occasionally as he looked for the right words.

Rascal watched the boy as he held the phone and listened in silence. His embarrassed expression slowly turned into a relieved smile.

'Thank you, Mrs Walker . . . Yes, yes, I'll see you next week!'

He put the phone down.

'Well?' said Lucas's dad.

'She said that she knew some money had gone missing as soon as she got into town. But she said there's no harm done now that I've told her the truth. I can drop the money off tomorrow and she wants me to carry on working in the garden next week.'

After that, Lucas's father prepared dinner, while Lucas checked Rascal's paw and bandaged it.

For the evening meal, Lucas and his dad sat opposite each other at the kitchen table. Rascal sat between them under the table and he ate his fill for the first time in many days.

As Rascal lay in the back garden after dinner, he felt tired but contented. He had run and played for a little while, but he knew that he needed to rest his injured paw. It was feeling a lot better now that it had been bandaged. He would have to give it a chance to heal fully before he hit the road again.

Well, there were worse places to stay for a day or two.

He closed his eyes and drifted off to the rhythmic sound of hands catching the ball.

Rascal's adventures aren't over yet.
Can he get home to his best friend Joel?
Read this special extract from

FACING THE FLAMES

to find out what happens next ...

CHAPTER 1

The sun had passed its noontime high point in the sky, but it still beat down fiercely. The shade of the forest offered Rascal little protection from its heat. Even the strong wind was hot and dry and gave no relief from the sun's rays.

More than anything in the world, Rascal wanted water right now – a long, cool drink of delicious water. He was hungry too, of course, but he could get along without food for now – he'd had a lot of practice at that recently, after all. But no living thing could survive long without water. If he didn't get a drink soon, he would be unable to take another step.

Many dogs would have stopped already; stopped and just lain down in the shade until the cool of the evening arrived. But Rascal would not give up. Whenever he felt as if he couldn't go on, the thought of who waited for him at journey's end spurred him on. Joel! It was the thought of his master, Joel, that had kept Rascal going for the hundreds of miles he had travelled so far. And it was the thought of Joel that would keep him going for the many miles that lay ahead too.

Now, if he could just find a drink of water . . .

He wasn't the only one thinking this way. It seemed that the whole forest around him was also crying out for water. It had struggled for too long without a drop of rain in this scorching summer. For days Rascal had thought that the drought would end, but somehow he always seemed to run ahead of the bank of clouds behind him to the east.

The evidence of the dry season was all around Rascal in the pale colours of the foliage. The lower branches of the trees were a dusty grey and the grasses and brush were more a washed-out yellow than a healthy green. Shrivelled brown leaves crackled beneath the dog's feet and brittle pine needles dug into the pads on his paws.

As he neared the ridge that ran along the top of this hill, he heard a sound above the noise of the wind. It was human voices, laughing. He could also hear the low crackle of a campfire and the smell of roasted meat.

Soon Rascal could see four people – two women and two men, all in their early twenties – sitting outside their badly pitched tents, which flapped precariously in the wind. One of the men was prodding a long stick into the campfire. Several objects wrapped in tinfoil sat in the fire.

'Don't think these potatoes are done yet,' said the man.

No one seemed to mind. They were all finishing off hamburgers, which had also been cooked on this fire (judging from the charred smell).

'Shouldn't we just have had something cold to eat?' said the woman with short red hair. 'I mean, it's hot enough already without having to light a fire.'

The man with the stick grinned. 'Listen, Debs. It isn't proper camping if you don't build a fire, is it?'

The other man, who had a scrubby beard, took a drink from a silver can and laughed. 'We never knew you were such a Boy Scout, Rick.'

The man with the stick did a silly salute with his free hand. 'Didn't you see me start this fire by rubbing two sticks together?'

'Course we did,' laughed the other woman, whose fair hair was pulled back into a ponytail. 'But I bet those matches in your pocket came in handy too!'

Rascal listened to them talking and joking for a few minutes more. He was waiting for clues, anything that might tell him if these people were the sort who would be kind to a stray dog like himself. His long, hard journey had taught Rascal only this about the behaviour of humans – some of them were wonderful and some of them were terrible, and many times you couldn't tell who was which until it was too late.

But his thirst wouldn't let him delay any longer. Rascal stood and pushed his way through the undergrowth towards the four people.

'Hey, look!' said the woman called Debs. 'It's a dog!'

'He could probably smell those burgers,' said the man with the beard. 'He must like *his* food burnt to a crisp as well!'

'He does look hungry,' said the second woman. 'Shall we give him something to eat?'

'No chance!' exclaimed Rick. 'If he wants a burger, he can go and buy his own, can't he?' He was holding the end of his stick in the heart of the campfire. After a few seconds he pulled it out, a flame now burning at the end. He waved it in Rascal's direction as if it were a sword. 'Clear off, wild beast!' he shouted, making his voice boom.

Rascal was tensed to run, but he could tell that the man was not really threatening him so much as trying to make his friends laugh.

'I don't think he reckons much to your flaming torch, Rick,' said Debs.

She was opening the top of a big plastic bottle of water. She poured a splash out to wash her hands.

Rascal couldn't help himself. When he saw that water he let out a little yap.

'Hold on, I don't think it *is* burgers he's after,' commented the woman with the ponytail. 'Look at him eyeing up that water. He wants a drink.'

'Can't blame him, in this heat,' said Debs. She poured some of the water into a plastic bowl and handed it to the man with the beard. 'Poor thing . . . Go on, give this to him.'

'Me? What if he's got rabies or

something?' complained the man. But he took the bowl and stood up.

Rascal watched his every step as he came closer.

The man took a drag on his cigarette and looked back at his friends. 'Tell you what,' he smirked. 'I'll give him a drink, but first he's got to do a few tricks. Fair enough?'